SUPER TURBO

VS. THE PENCIL POINTER

By Lee Kirby

Illustrated by George O'Connor

LITTLE SIMON

New York   London   Toronto   Sydney   New Delhi

LITTLE SIMON

An imprint of Simon & Schuster Children's Publishing Division • 1230 Avenue of the Americas, New York, New York 10020 • First Little Simon paperback edition July 2017. Copyright © 2017 by Simon & Schuster, Inc. All rights reserved, including the right of reproduction in whole or in part in any form. LITTLE SIMON is a registered trademark of Simon & Schuster, Inc., and associated colophon is a trademark of Simon & Schuster, Inc. For information about special discounts for bulk purchases, please contact Simon & Schuster Special Sales at 1-866-506-1949 or business@simonandschuster.com. The Simon & Schuster Speakers Bureau can bring authors to your live event. For more information or to book an event contact the Simon & Schuster Speakers Bureau at 1-866-248-3049 or visit our website at www.simonspeakers.com. Designed by Jay Colvin. The text of this book was set in Little Simon Gazette.

Manufactured in the United States of America 0517 MTN 10 9 8 7 6 5 4 3 2 1 Cataloging-in-Publication Data for this title is available from the Library of Congress.

ISBN 978-1-4814-9439-7 (hc)
ISBN 978-1-4814-9438-0 (pbk)
ISBN 978-1-4814-9440-3 (eBook)

CONTENTS

1

A VISITOR IN CLASSROOM C

What is this big secret, you might ask? We'll get to that. For now, Sunnyview Elementary School is just your typical old elementary school. And Classroom C of Sunnyview Elementary School is just your typical second-grade classroom.

STUDENTS ENJOYING THEIR FREE READING TIME? TYPICAL.

THEIR TEACHER, MS. BEASLEY, GRADING PAPERS? TYPICAL.

THE DESKS? THE CHALKBOARD? THE BOOKSHELVES? TYPICAL.

TURBO!

EVERYTHING WAS COMPLETELY TYPICAL . . . EXCEPT FOR THIS GUY RIGHT HERE.

Oh sure, Turbo might *look* like an ordinary hamster. But remember that big secret? Well, here it is. You see, Turbo *isn't* an ordinary hamster. He's also . . . Super Turbo, the mightiest super-hamster in the entire known universe!

But the students of Classroom C have no idea that Turbo is a super-hamster. And Turbo has to protect his secret identity. So around the kids, Turbo is just typical Turbo. That's okay with him because being the official pet of Classroom C is a big duty and even superheroes enjoy some time off!

RING-A-DING-DING!

The bell sounded the end of the school day. Some of the students filed past Turbo's cage and waved to him on their way out.

Ms. Beasley spent a few minutes gathering up her things, and then she left too. "Good night, Turbo, see you tomorrow!" she called as she shut the door behind her.

What to do? thought Turbo. He didn't have any plans tonight since there was no Superpet Superhero League meeting on the schedule.

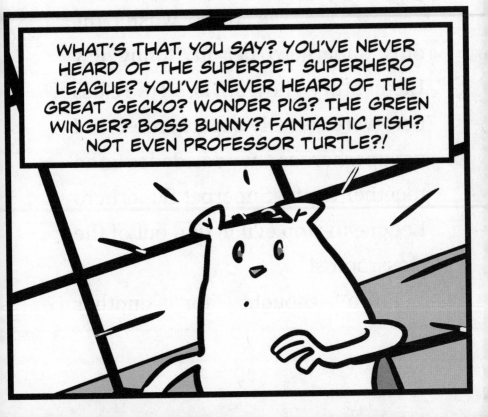

Well then, read closely! You see, Turbo wasn't the only superhero pet in Sunnyview Elementary. The truth is, *all* the class pets were secretly superheroes. And as superheroes, they decided to band together as the Superpet Superhero League to stop evil in and out of the classrooms!

Turbo thought for another

moment about his plans. Suddenly, he knew what he was going to do for the rest of the night. He climbed onto his water bottle and gently lifted the top of his cage. Then he swung down from the table and scurried across the floor to the reading nook. He'd been reading a Rider Woofson adventure the past few nights and he was anxious to see how it ended.

Turbo settled in and was leisurely reading when . . .

CLICK!

What was that noise?

CREAK!

Turbo looked toward the door. Oh no! It was opening! Which meant . . . someone was about to enter Classroom C!

Turbo looked around for a hiding spot.

A foot entered the classroom. Turbo dove underneath his book, hoping it would cover him.

Then he had a horrible thought— what if whoever it was noticed that Turbo wasn't in his cage? *They'll think I've been kidnapped! They'll send out search parties!*

Turbo dared to peek out of his hiding place. He breathed a sigh of relief when he saw that the mysterious visitor was just the school janitor. He was probably coming to empty the trash.

But wait! He wasn't heading for the trash! He was heading directly for Turbo's cage!

The janitor stood in front of Turbo's cage. Then he opened his

supply kit and pulled something out. What was it? Turbo strained his eyes but it was too far away to see.

Suddenly there came an awful

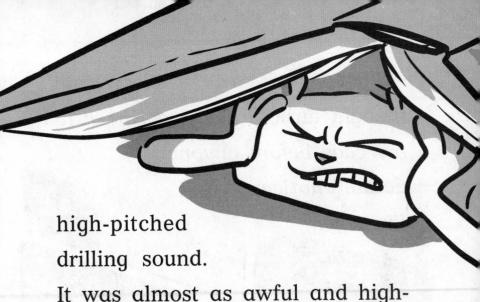

high-pitched
drilling sound.
It was almost as awful and high-pitched as the alarm in the cafeteria, which Turbo had set off one time in order to defeat an evil rat named Whiskerface.

And then it was over. The janitor packed up his things and headed for the door. He flicked off the lights as he left.

Phew! That was a close call!
thought Turbo. *I better get back to
my cage before anyone
actually notices
I'm gone.*

It took Turbo a while to get back in the dark, and when he finally did, he was relieved to see that everything looked normal. But . . . if everything looked normal, then what was the janitor doing?

②

THE BIG REVEAL!

Turbo opened his eyes. Sunlight was streaming in through the classroom windows. He got up, yawned, and stretched. Had last night been all a dream? Turbo looked around. On the shelf above his cage, he could see . . . *something*. So it hadn't been a dream. Whatever the janitor had installed last night was up there, but Turbo sure couldn't tell what it was.

Was it a machine that shot out laser nets any time a kid picked his nose? Or a freeze ray if someone whispered in class? Or a top secret ghost detector? The possibilities were endless!

Turbo was just about to climb up onto his water bottle and take a closer look when . . .

RING-A-DING-DING!

Students began to file into Classroom C. Turbo would have to wait until later to see what was up there.

Ms. Beasley was making an announcement at the head of the classroom.

Oh good, thought Turbo, *she knows all about the mysterious device! She's probably going to warn the kids to stay clear until it can be properly removed from the shelf above my hamster cage.*

"Class, I just wanted to point out," Ms. Beasley was saying, "that we have an exciting new addition to the classroom!" She gestured toward Turbo's cage. "A brand-new electric pencil sharpener!" she announced.

The class *oohed* and *aahed* as if Ms. Beasley had just revealed that it was a flying chocolate-maker.

A hand shot up. It was a girl named Meredith whom Turbo had been keeping an eye on. The word in the Superpet Superhero League was that she was a potential troublemaker.

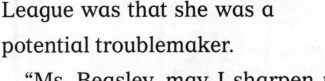

"Ms. Beasley, may I sharpen my pencil?" Meredith asked.

"Yes, Meredith," Ms. Beasley replied. "Anytime anyone needs to sharpen their pencil, they may get up and do so quietly."

Meredith sprang up and ran to the sharpener.

It was awful. Turbo would have covered his ears, but with Meredith right there, all the kids would've probably noticed, and then they'd start asking questions, and then he'd have to reveal his secret identity, and then . . . it was too risky.

Meredith pulled her pencil out of the sharpener and held it up. "Pointy!" she proclaimed.

Pretty soon, the whole class had lined up to sharpen their pencils.

*Why is everyone so excited about
a pencil sharpener?* thought Turbo.
*Can't they just chew their pencils
into points, like I can?*

Turbo never got his answer.
Instead, the pencil sharpening
continued. NONSTOP. ALL DAY.

Turbo sat grumpily in his cage,
food pellets in his ears to block
out the noise. But toward the end
of the day, Turbo began to notice

something. And that something was falling into his cage. It looked like his cedar chips, but it was lighter and fluffier.

Then Turbo let out a gasp. It was pencil shavings!

The pencil sharpener was dropping pencil shavings into Turbo's cage! Every time a kid sharpened their pencil, a few more flakes fell down! At this rate Turbo was surely going to be buried!

EMERGENCY MEETING!

"I suppose you're all wondering why I called this emergency meeting of the Superpet Superhero League," said Super Turbo.

School had let out a few hours ago. Now the class pets were gathered in their secret meeting place, the reading nook of Classroom C.

Super Turbo brushed a few pencil shavings off his cape. "Something strange is happening in Classroom C," he continued.

"That's funny," said a parakeet named Clever, who was also known as the Green Winger. "Something strange is happening in Classroom D as well!"

"Weird," said Leo, the official pet of Classroom A, also known as the Great Gecko. "I was going to report strange happenings in my

classroom as well!"

"Me too!" exclaimed Angelina the guinea pig, who also known as Wonder Pig. She was the official pet of Classroom B.

"This . . . is . . . mysterious . . . ," Warren said as slowly as you'd expect a turtle to speak. He was the class pet of the science lab, and he was also known as Professor Turtle.

"What's going on?" asked Nell from within the water-filled Turbo-mobile that served as her home when she wasn't in her fish tank. She was also known as Fantastic Fish.

LAST NIGHT THE JANITOR CAME IN HERE, AND HE SCREWED SOMETHING IN.

I COULDN'T SEE WHAT IT WAS BECAUSE HE TURNED OFF THE LIGHTS WHEN HE LEFT.

BUT IN THE MORNING, THE EVIL THING REVEALED ITSELF.

AND IT'S ... AN ELECTRIC PENCIL SHARPENER!

AND THAT'S NOT ALL! THE PENCIL SHAVINGS ARE FALLING INTO MY CAGE, AND IF WE DON'T STOP THIS THING, IT'S GOING TO BURY ME ALIVE!

"Hmm . . . ," said Frank, also known as Boss Bunny. He was the official pet of the principal's office. "And you're telling me this happened in every classroom last night?"

The Green Winger, Wonder Pig, and the Great Gecko all nodded.

"How could the janitor be so careless?" asked Super Turbo.

"What if . . . ," began Boss Bunny, "what if the janitor *wasn't* being careless?"

"Hold on. Who—or *what*—is the *Pencil Pointer*?" asked Fantastic Fish, scratching her head with her fin.

"I think you'd better come with me," said Boss Bunny darkly. "There's something you all need to see."

4

A POINTY PLAN

The superpets followed Boss Bunny to the vent in Classroom C.

Using her super-pig strength, Wonder Pig removed the vent cover and the animals filed inside.

When the Superpet Superhero League had formed, they'd decided that the best way to travel in secret

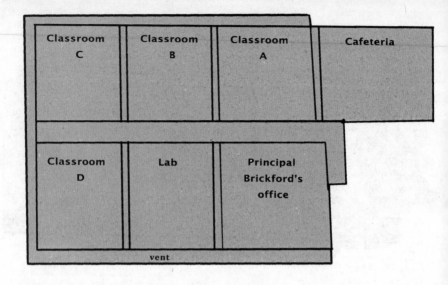

was to use the vent system. It was also their way of communicating. Each pet had an object that they hid just inside the vent in their classroom. They'd tap it on the vent floor, and the sound would echo throughout the whole system. Turbo's object was that ruler right there.

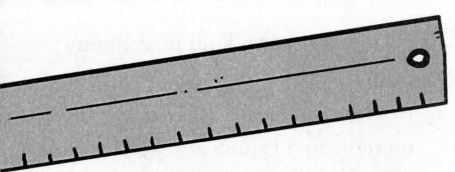

Being a guinea pig, Wonder Pig not only had strength, but also super maze-running abilities. The superpets followed her as she raced through the vents. She popped out into each classroom to make sure that, yes, the Pencil Pointer had indeed struck each and every one!

Now the Superpets climbed out of the vent that led into Principal Baxter Brickford's office.

"It's over here," said Boss Bunny, taking the lead. "On Principal Brickford's desk." He led all the animals to a yellow notepad.

ARE THOSE ALL DRAWINGS OF YOU?

OH—ER—YES, I GUESS SO. WHAT CAN I SAY? PRINCIPAL BRICKFORD'S A BIG FAN OF MINE.

BUT LOOK! IT'S A MAP! AND IN EACH CLASSROOM . . .

"Boss Bunny, you're sounding a little like our old enemy Whisker-face," said Fantastic Fish. "How does installing a pencil sharpener in each classroom help the Pencil Pointer take over the school?"

"Excellent question!" said Boss Bunny. "First, have you noticed how the kids are mesmerized by these pencil sharpeners?"

"Yes!" exclaimed Super Turbo. "Is it mind control?"

"It very well could be, Super Turbo," said Boss Bunny. "These kids keep sharpening and sharpening and SHARPENING their pencils—"

The Great Gecko snapped his fingers. "Until we're all buried beneath a mountain of pencil shavings!"

"And then there are no superpets to protect the school!" cried Wonder Pig with a gasp.

"Exactly," replied Boss Bunny. "We can't expect the kids and teachers to understand the danger they're in. And with no superpets around, the Pencil Pointer will easily take control of Sunnyview

Elementary School!"

"But *who* is the Pencil Pointer?" asked Wonder Pig, scratching her head. "Is it Principal Brickford?"

"It can't be," said the Green Winger, pointing at the drawings of Boss Bunny. "The Pencil Pointer wants to get *rid* of the school pets, and Principal Brickford clearly loves Frank."

Boss Bunny giggled with delight, then got serious. "It must be someone *above* Principal Brickford! Someone who hates cute, fuzzy animals!"

The Great Gecko leaned forward. "What does it say there toward the bottom of the map?"

Trial in Cafeteria

Super Turbo adjusted his goggles. "It says 'trial in cafeteria.'"

"Well . . . that's . . . mysterious" said Professor Turtle.

"Are you guys thinking what I'm thinking?" asked Wonder Pig.

5

SNACK ATTACK!

The Superpet Superhero League arrived at the school cafeteria.

"I know we came here for snacks, but maybe we'll find some clues about this mysterious Pencil Pointer too," said Turbo.

"And maybe we'll find some nacho cheese potato chips!" said

Wonder Pig, licking her lips.

"And some gummy worms!" said the Green Winger. "Way better than real worms!" she added. "Believe me, I would know!"

In the pantry the Great Gecko used his sticky hands and feet and

his super climbing power to scale the side of the cabinet where the snacks were kept.

GASP!

WHAT IS IT? ANOTHER TRAP FROM THE PENCIL POINTER?!

NO! IT'S EVEN WORSE! THE SNACKS . . . THEY'RE GONE!

The superpets looked around. The Great Gecko was right. The snack cupboard was completely bare!

"Maybe check the fridge?" called out Fantastic Fish.

"Good idea!" yelled the Great Gecko. He scurried over to the fridge.

Suddenly the superpets heard a loud whistle. They whirled around.

Slowly, creeping out from the shadows, stepped . . .

"What—what do you have there?" Fantastic Fish stammered, practically drooling with hunger.

"Oh, this?" asked Whiskerface, stroking his long whiskers. "This is just a bag of incredibly delicious nacho cheese potato chips. The *last* bag of incredibly delicious nacho cheese potato chips in the whole school. And maybe even in the whole world!"

6

CAFETERIA SHOWDOWN

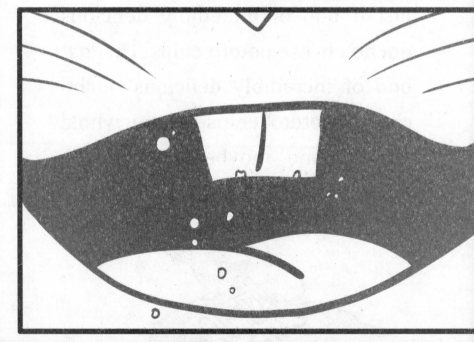

Whiskerface paced back and forth, showing off his goods. "You super*pests* shouldn't even bother looking for the good snacks. My Rat Packers cleaned out the whole cupboard!" He laughed his evil squeaky laugh.

"I can't . . . believe . . . it!" said

Professor Turtle. "Whiskerface . . . is the . . . Pencil Pointer!"

"But now you've taken our snacks!" said Wonder Pig, cracking her knuckles. "Now you've gone too far!"

Whiskerface stood there blinking his beady eyes. "Yeah, sure, I'm totally the, uh, Pointy Pencil guy. You got me."

"Wait, guys!" cried Super Turbo, leaping forward. "Remember what it said on the map? 'Trial in cafeteria'?"

"Yeah . . . that surely was . . . mysterious," said Professor Turtle.

WELL, CLEARLY WHISKERFACE ISN'T THE PENCIL POINTER! HE CAN'T EVEN SAY THE NAME RIGHT!

I AM TOO THE PUNKY POINTY!

"I don't know what you pooper-pets are talking about," said Whiskerface. "But I think you're all crazy." He started to back away. "You've not heard the last of the Pinky Pusher!" he cried as he dove through the hole in the wall that led to his lair.

The superpets approached the bag of potato chips Whiskerface had left behind.

"Is there anything in there?" asked Super Turbo. "Are they . . . "

Professor Turtle looked up sadly. "Gone."

With a sob, Boss Bunny threw himself onto his belly, shoveling pawfuls of potato chip dust into his mouth.

Wonder Pig and the Great Gecko grabbed him by the arms and

dragged him away. "It's okay, Boss
Bunny. Let it go. Just let it go."

Super Turbo clenched his fists.
Whoever this Pencil Pointer was, he
was going to pay!

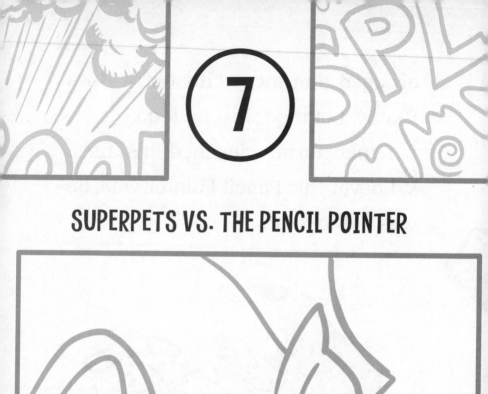

SUPERPETS VS. THE PENCIL POINTER

The superpets sadly made their way back to Classroom C. Super Turbo was pretty sure he could even hear Boss Bunny sniffling a little.

As the pets exited the vent into the classroom, Super Turbo looked up at the pencil sharpener. It was just sitting there, above his cage.

Staring at him. It almost looked like it was . . . smiling?

Using every last bit of his super-hamster speed, Super Turbo bounded up to his cage. With a mighty leap, he practically flew up to the shelf where the pencil sharpener was bolted. But he didn't have enough strength to pull himself up!

He was starting to lose his grip!

"Come on, guys!" shouted the Great Gecko, springing into action. "We have to get up there and help Super Turbo!" Then he looked around. "Well, those of us who *can* actually get up there."

The Great Gecko scampered up the wall while the Green Winger flew over to the shelf. The other animals cheered them on from below.

They each grabbed one of Super Turbo's arms and pulled him onto the shelf. Together, the trio tried to knock the pencil sharpener out of place.

"It's bolted down tight!" grunted Super Turbo. "We need more force!"

BOSS BUNNY! DO YOU HAVE ANYTHING IN YOUR UTILITY BELT THAT WILL TAKE CARE OF THESE SCREWS?

HMM, I HAVE THIS PIECE OF LICORICE, THAT MIGHT—

NO, MAYBE THIS ERASER?

UH, TIC TAC?

THIS IS GETTING US NOWHERE FAST!

ONE, TWO, THREE!

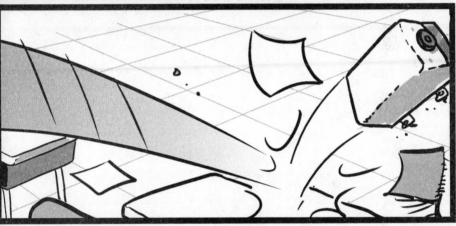

8

ONE DOWN

Super Turbo, Wonder Pig, and the Great Gecko made their way down from the shelf. Then they lay on the floor, exhausted. They had defeated the pencil sharpener, but it had taken everything they had. And there were still plenty more sharpeners out there!

Fantastic Fish, Boss Bunny,

Professor Turtle, and the Green Winger came over to check on them.

"Are you all right?" Fantastic Fish asked Super Turbo. Super Turbo gave a thumbs-up. The Great Gecko managed to nod. And the Green Winger waved a wing.

"Good," said Fantastic Fish. "You guys really sent that pencil sharpener flying!"

"It was . . . awesome!" Professor Turtle cried.

"Nice work," Boss Bunny agreed.

"Definitely," said the Green Winger. "But we should probably go make sure nothing got broken."

The superpets made their way over to the reading nook, where the pencil sharpener had landed.

"Looks like the pencil sharpener is still in one piece," noted Fantastic Fish.

Super Turbo nodded. A few books had gotten knocked over and there were pencil shavings scattered about, but there was no other damage.

Then Super Turbo noticed something else. It was a piece of paper that seemed to have fallen onto the floor.

OOH, A DRAWING!

A REALLY POINTY PENCIL?

Super Turbo looked down at the drawing. He suddenly felt really guilty. The kids of Classroom C had been *so* excited about the pencil sharpener.

"Guys, what if this *wasn't* some sinister plan crafted by the mysterious Pencil Pointer?"

Super Turbo and the superpets knew what they had to do. They cleaned up the reading nook. Then they worked together to get the pencil sharpener up on Ms. Beasley's desk so she'd see it first thing when she came in.

Their job done, the superpets made their way to the vent so they could return to their respective classrooms.

As he left, Boss Bunny turned back to Super Turbo. "Just one more thing," he said. "If the Pencil Pointer isn't real, then what is that map I showed you guys? And what does 'trial in the cafeteria' mean?"

Super Turbo shook his head. "I don't know, Boss Bunny. But right now, I think we all need some rest." And with that, Super Turbo climbed into his cage and fell into a deep sleep.

9

AND IT WAS ALL WORTH IT

The next morning plain, old, typical Turbo looked out on his plain,
old, typical classroom in plain, old
Sunnyview Elementary School. He
smiled.

Earlier Ms. Beasley had arrived
and found the pencil sharpener on
her desk. Which had led her to look

at where the pencil sharpener was
supposed to be, on the shelf above
Turbo's cage. Which had led her to
notice Turbo's cage. Which had led

her to realize that the pencil shavings from the pencil sharpener had
been falling *into* Turbo's cage!

Ms. Beasley had the janitor come

in and reinstall the pencil sharpener, this time on the corner of her
own desk.

RING-A-DING-DING!

"Okay, class," said Ms. Beasley when all the students were seated. "I have a few announcements this morning. First, I'm supposed to tell you that tomorrow we will be starting a trial in the cafeteria."

Turbo's ears perked up at the sound of this. Trial? Cafeteria?

"We're doing a trial run of great new snacks such as organic fruits and vegetables, gluten-free bread, hummus, and all kinds of yummy stuff," explained Ms. Beasley.

A boy in the back of the room raised his hand. "You're not getting rid of the old snacks too, are you?" he asked. "I'm on a very strict all-cheese diet."

Ms. Beasley laughed. "No, Charlie," she told the boy. "After this

trial, we'll be stocking the cafeteria with all sorts of delicious *and* healthy snacks."

At this, the class gave a cheer.

In his cage Turbo chuckled to himself. So *that* was the trial in the cafeteria! Mystery solved! Wait until he told the rest of the Superpet Superhero League!

Then Ms. Beasley told the students about how the pencil sharpener had been raining pencil shavings on poor Turbo, and how she'd had it reinstalled on her desk.

This time a different boy from the back of the room raised his hand. "Ms. Beasley, I feel really bad about making it rain pencil shavings on Turbo," he said. "Do you think we could all make it up to him by drawing pictures of him? That might show Turbo how special he is to us!"

"What a wonderful idea, Eugene!" Ms. Beasley exclaimed.

In his cage Turbo beamed.

At Ms. Beasley's desk the students lined up to sharpen their pencils.

For some reason, the sound wasn't so bad this time!

Then the kids spent the morning drawing pictures of their beloved classroom pet.

Turbo sat back in his cage, surrounded by all the beautiful drawings made for him by the students of Classroom C.

It was certainly hard work being the official pet of a second-grade classroom, and even *more* work being a superhero. But it sure was worth it.

IF YOU LIKE SUPER TURBO, YOU'LL LOVE DOG DETECTIVE RIDER WOOFSON! HERE'S A PEEK AT THE FIRST BOOK:

Rider Woofson stared out of his office window, looking over the city skyline. Buildings stretched out for miles in every direction. This was Pawston, the animal capital of the world. Every day, thousands of animals went about their business, behaving as good citizens should.

But this city also had a darker side, known as the criminal underbelly. And it was not the kind of belly you wanted to scratch. Not unless you wanted to get bit!

That was where Rider Woofson came in. Rider was no ordinary canine. He was the greatest dog detective in Pawston—maybe even the world. And with the help of his pals in the Pup Investigators Pack, criminals didn't stand a chance.

In fact, the only problem for the P.I. Pack was waiting for an actual crime to happen.

"Well, it's been a pretty quiet afternoon, huh, Boss?" said Westie Barker.

"It is quiet," Rider woofed. "Too quiet." He fixed his crooked tie and adjusted his hat. "I don't like it."

"A day off must be *terrier*-fying for a working dog like you," the West Highland terrier said with a laugh. He was fiddling with a screwdriver and what used to be a vacuum cleaner. "Try to enjoy it. You could grab a dognap or buy a new collar. Maybe play a game of fetch?"

"We're not pups anymore," Rider

said, looking over his friend's shoulder. "Say, what is that?"

"It's my new toy project . . . a jetpack!" Westie said as he wagged his tail. The white-furred terrier was a true gadget expert. He was always building something new. "With this strapped to my back, I'll be able to solve crimes faster than a speeding greyhound."

"I bet that jetpack won't get one foot off the ground," Rora Gooddog said from across the room. She was the slickest poodle on the block, and twice as smart. She was sitting at her desk, writing up a crime report.

"Flying is for the birds anyways," said a floppy-haired mutt named Ziggy Fluffenscruff. "I like to keep my paws on the ground, thank you very much." The young pup sniffed around the office. He followed his nose over to the file cabinet. After digging through a few papers, he pulled out a bone and hugged it. *"Bow-wowza!"* he yipped. "I knew you weren't lost."

"So you're the one who put bite marks on this," Rora said as she grabbed the bone back and returned it to the file cabinet. "This is evidence, not dinner. Now, quit thinking with your stomach."

"Thinking with my stomach has helped solve lots of cases, you know," Ziggy whispered to himself, curling up on the couch. "Like that one with the mean dog magician, Labra-cadabra-dor."

"Kid, you've got a real talent there," Rider said. "And I bet your nose could smell trouble a mile away."

LEE KIRBY has the proportionate strength and abilities of a man-size hamster. He spends his days chewing up cardboard and running in giant plastic bubbles throughout his very own fortress of solitude in Brooklyn, New York. And, no, he is not related to world-famous Captain Awesome author Stan Kirby. Or is he?

GEORGE O'CONNOR is the creator of the *New York Times* bestselling graphic novel series Olympians, in addition to serving as the illustrator of the Captain Awesome series. He is also the author and illustrator of the picture books *Kapow!*, *Ker-splash*, and *If I Had a Triceratops*. He resides in his secret Brooklyn, New York, hideout, where he uses his amazing artistic powers to strike fear in the hearts of bad guys everywhere!